Mental Illness Put into Words

Miranda L. Soares

Dedicated to:

First of all, I want to thank my brothers and sisters for making sure that I never gave up along the way.

Also, I dedicate this book to my teachers because without them I probably would not have made it this far.

Thank you to my friends for editing this book. Without your critique or admiration, I possibly would have given up, and a special thanks to C. S. for the images.

Mostly, I dedicate this to my parents for always believing and pushing me forward and making me who I am today.

I love you. Thank you so much for all that you've done.

Table of Contents

The illness in this upcoming story is not very prominent, but it plays a small part on the plot — pushing things forward.

Story One: Lost in Time

I woke up in a dark room, the scent of vanilla and lavender hitting my nose. Beside me, sat a female — her dark hair long and in her face — just staring at me. She was clothed in a Victorian style dress. I remember this place, vaguely. She stood up and walked over to where I sat. With a smile on her face, she raised her hand, and that's when I noticed the piece of ham she had in her grasp. With a loud, creepy laugh, she flung the ham at me.

My eyes shot open, and I was met with a blinding light. My vision was blurred. I tried to remember where I actually was. My head started spinning, and I was unable to move my arms to which I realized were strapped to my chest. I let out a laugh. I finally got that special jacket where I could hug myself. Then, I thought, "There is only one way I would be able to get this vest. But why am I in a mental hospital?" My head started hurting as I tried to remember.

A man dressed in a white lab coat walked into the room. With a small smile on his face, he walked over to me. I had a strange feeling that he was here to hurt me, or at least, hopefully to explain what I was doing here in this padded room. "So, you're awake. Do you remember how you got here?" he asked.

I rolled my eyes. "I thought you could tell me."

He ignored my rude comment and helped me to my feet. "We're sorry for having to put you in this empty and plain room." His voice was calm, and full of faux care. "I'm going to take you to the therapist to see if she can help you remember what happened."

"Whatever," I muttered. The feeling had returned, though it had not completely left me. Now, things felt as if I didn't want to know how I actually got here. Were things really that bad that I had to block them out? Maybe nothing was wrong, but...they are here to make me think something is. Maybe...that could explain a lot. This explains why I couldn't remember and why I woke up here without remembering even going to bed.

I glanced at the man that walked beside me and asked, "By the way, what's your name?"

"My name? Well, you can just call me Dr. White," he answered with a chuckle.

"Dr. White," I thought, "how…fitting." He led me to a pale room — not exactly white, but it didn't have enough color to be called peach. In the center of the room sat a young woman, no older than in her thirties, in a short skimpy dress. My eye twitched. I thought that working in a place like this meant wearing clothes that didn't show as much skin, but I could be wrong.

Dr. White gave this lady a nod then quickly left. The scent of vanilla and lavender had returned, and I was reminded of the dream I had. The more I thought about it, the lady in my dream could have represented this woman…or I could just be thinking too much.

I continued to stare at the lady in front of me who sat at her desk. I wondered about the Victorian dress, "Is this what they mean by Victoria's Secret?" When I let out a loud and obnoxious laugh, the therapist gave me a strange look — the one that teachers give students, where they question the stability of your sanity. I used to get that look all the time from my family. MY FAMILY! Are they worried about me? What are they doing right now?

As I stood there thinking about everything, the therapist jotted everything I did on a small notepad. After a few minutes of me just standing there, she stood up and walked over to me.

"Would you like to get started now?" she asked.

I narrowed my eyes. "Sure... Can you tell me how I got here?"

She walked me over to a couch that faced her desk, both of which were a very bright, almost white color. "Why is everything so bland?"

After making sure I was comfortable, she went back to her chair, pulling it close to the couch. "Close your eyes," she said.

I rolled my eyes before closing them, doing as she asked. "Why am I here?"

"When we...when we found you, three days ago, you were bloodied, surrounded by lifeless bodies, and covered in self-inflicted wounds."

It seemed like everything froze. Lifeless bodies...self-inflicted wounds...? Then, after what felt like hours, it all came back to me. I was able to remember how I got here, and what happened before all of it. I was right earlier; I did not want to remember how I got here.

"By that look on your face, I believe you remember what happened. What we are here for today is to talk about why you did what you did."

The air grew thick and it became harder for me to breathe. The reality of it all came crashing down on me. My family...my family is dead, and it's because of me. My paranoia returned. If I tell Dr. Black (I finally remembered her name!) what really happened, they could put me away for life. Then again, if I stay quiet, they could still put me away, for lying and withholding information. Either way, I was screwed. I might as well get it off my chest.

"Tell me what you remember, we can help." She started.

I nodded slightly. Now that I actually remembered it, I realized that none of it made sense. I felt a tear escape and slide down my cheek. "I had to! They were planning against me!" I pulled my knees up to my chest and wrapped my arms around my legs. I thought back to what happened.

We had had a family reunion; we came together and met up at the nearest beach, Leaf Star Beach. Several cousins of mine dragged me away. I remember it being around midnight, but much of it was hazy. There was alcohol, and though we were all of age, they had to sneak it past the others. Also there was weed, if I remembered correctly.

I recalled all that I could to Dr. Black, going against my better judgment. For a moment, I felt that there was more than just Dr. Black listening to my story, but I shook it off.

Most of my relatives did not hold their liquor well, so I should have known that things were going to be bad. If I had known what was actually going to happen, I would have left. I would have gone to get some help before — If only I had known earlier — because I am now in some deep trouble.

Everyone that had been around the campfire that night was plastered. My doctor had told me not to take alcohol with the medication or while on it. When I told Dr. Black about this, she questioned what type of medication and what was it used for.

"Um…" My eye began twitching. I couldn't remember. "I don't remember. He said it was for per…persecutory paranoia. But while I was there, I wasn't on the medication. I had run out of refills and while the pharmacy was trying to get a hold of my doctor, I went without." Even now I was going without the medication.

She wrote this down. "We'll have to get a hold of your doctor."

Dr. Black said some stuff that made me believe that they did not know as much about me as I thought, or they were pretending to act like that to make me think they did not know about me…I clenched my eyes tighter. Why does it seem like everyone is against me?

"There was a boar…a pig…that set it off. After it attacked us, I went off on the others. They had thought that I was playing, messing with them. I started yelling at them and throwing things.

"The next thing I remembered, the sun was rising and so were the others. But my cousins — the traitors, the ones that were at the bonfire the night before — would never rise again. The drying blood was across my hands and on my clothes. It was almost dried, crusted and discolored. I was unable to remember how it happened, but I did know that it was because of me.

"As I went through the rest of the day, it felt as if my paranoia overtook me. It felt like each of them were planning on harming me, and they were all my enemies. My subconscious, the voice in my head, continued to push me; I told myself over and over that this was the only thing I could do to save myself. I could blame the influence of the drugs or alcohol, or even me being paranoid over every little thing, but it wouldn't matter. No one would believe me."

Dr. Black closed her notepad with a sad smile on her face. "It is enough that you know what happened. If it means anything, I believe you."

I rolled my eyes and turned to stare at her. I knew what she said, all of it, were lies. Therapists really don't care about anything their patients tell them. I had learned that over that past few years, as a result of sessions before and after my psychotherapy classes. I had to get out of here. I was not feeling safe in this place.

The intercom overhead buzzed. "Lunch time. Now, let's get you out of this. It was simply a precaution as the other doctors helped you in here." Dr. Black stood up and helped me out of my vest, letting my arms free. I thought over everything and wondered, "Why was I in the jacket in the first place. Did I try to take my own life three days ago?" This, I still could not remember.

But it didn't matter; the only thing I cared about was escaping this place. It would not be so hard. I thought I would be able to outsmart all of the guards here, and I did.

As they transported me from the therapy room to the lunch room, I slipped out of Dr. White's grasp and took off running. Though, not putting much thought into the plan, I was able to break free. I just continued to run, never stopping, never second-guessing my not-thought-out plan, and not letting the others catch up. They ran after me, wanting to catch me, but my want to get out of this place was greater, much greater.

Somehow, I was able to escape the hospital grounds, not stopping until I reached the edge of the ocean. So we're still on Leaf Star Island? I didn't know if this was good…or bad.

I didn't care, neither did the flying unicorn that floated overhead. I blinked and did a double-take. Wow! What kind of drugs did they give me while I was there?

What felt like a bucket of water was poured on me. I shrieked and sat up in the bed. Wait, a bed? I looked around and noticed I wasn't in a bed per say, but more of a sleeping bag.

"Come on little cousin. Let's go," said my older cousin as he stood over me, his eyes glossy. Was he already wasted? I glanced around and saw that I was back in the tent, at the family reunion! I did a victory dance in my head, glad none of that happened.

Then I blacked out.

When I came to, I was on my knees, leaning over the dead body of my cousin. I blinked. "No...No...NO!" I screamed. "Not again, please no!"

It’s Too Much

Hiding in the corners of the corridors

Sneaking right under your nose

It’s the nervous wreck, your nervous soul

They're there to catch you

There to harm you

They are your enemies

Your foes

Run! Hide! Turn left! Turn right!

It's your paranoia

Your mind

You keep running and hiding

Till finally

Your mind swallows you whole.

There are different types of depression. The one being focused on in the following story is "Post-Partum Depression" which was brought on from issues the character had with her own mother.

Story Two: A Second Chance

They say everything in life happens for a reason. Sometimes something so little can affect you in a large way. I recently learned this the hard way.

Everything was going great until I saw him. I swerved to the right — barely missing him — but ran off the road. The erratic movement of the turn caused the vehicle to slide and start rolling down the hill. I clenched my eyes shut as I hoped for the best. When the car stopped, I let out a breath, believing the worst was over. I opened my eyes, only to find myself not in the driver's seat where I had been, but rather standing in the grass a few yards away. Beside me stood a figure I had thought about so many times before, Death.

Death stood like a statue, dressed in a simple black cloak. I stared at the mess, hoping this was all a dream.

"Why are you here?" I asked in a whisper. "My life has just begun…" He didn't answer.

He turned around and started walking away. Actually, it wasn't walking...what he did was more like floating away. My eyes darted to the upside-down car then over to where Death was going; after a moment I darted after him. "Wait, so how does this work?" He kept walking and soon we were standing in a white hallway.

The stench of antiseptics filled the air and I shuttered. We walked down the corridor and I was looking at everyone and everything. I followed him into an elevator a little confused.

"If we were able to get here in the blink of an eye...why do we have to use the elevator?" He turned his head toward me; I could feel his stare burn a hole in the side of my head as I watched the elevator doors. The doors finally opened and Death stepped out while I followed close behind.

We walked down the halls when he stopped suddenly, causing me to almost crash into the back of him. I glanced at the door then back to the Grim Reaper next to me. I had this strange feeling of foreboding, a persistent emotion of dread. This room... I had no idea what waited for us behind this door, but I didn't want to see it. I tried to walk away but he pushed me through the open door.

Inside, the first thing I noticed was how pale I looked, how weak I had become, so frail...I looked so close to death lying in that hospital bed. There were bloody bandages wrapped around my wrists. "Why am I here? Why do I look like that?"

He shook his head and replied "You know why...Before your body prepared to die, your soul was already dying."

"My soul?" I questioned.

"Yes, that part of you that loves...the part that cares...The part of you that wants to go on."

As harsh as that sounded, he was absolutely right. I had already stopped caring about work and the rest of my friends. But this made me wonder, how far in my future is this? Why am I lying in that bed alone? "Where is my husband? Where are my kids?"

"I think you know that too."

I couldn't understand what he meant by that, but I began feeling dizzy. I collapsed and before I knew it the scene around me had changed, and I was back in my own house. Things here felt the same but...still so empty. I walked into the living room, noticing myself on the couch, sobbing. There were tears running down her...my cheeks. I dashed out of the room, not able to see her in such a mess. Running upstairs I realized I had yet to see the kids. It wasn't until moments later that I knew why. Their room was completely empty.

"Are they gone?"

He shook his head. "In a sense. Not like dead, as you're thinking...Your husband hated seeing you in such a mess. He tried to get you some help, but you shrugged it off, saying you were fine. After a while, he gave up and took the kids."

"What made him finally leave?"

"You stayed locked up, ignoring the rest of the world. He couldn't take care of the kids by himself plus a needy and emotionless wife. He took the kids one day and just disappeared."

Tears started to run down my own cheeks and I covered my face with my hands, wiping the tears away. Everything changed and Death and I were now sitting in the backseat of my car, where this all started.

"What were you thinking before I interrupted?" he asked.

"I was thinking about my daughter. She's about a month old. I should feel ecstatic about being a new mother, but I feel like I did when I was a child... I fear that I might be like my mother who left me with my aunt so she could get on with her life. I felt the same emptiness now, watching my own baby, as I did when I was a child myself."

He nodded. "You're mother left you as a child?"

"Yes, she abandoned me with my horrible aunt for all those years of misery. She had no room for a child in her life, so she left me alone. I have never forgiven her for that. The sad thing is...I never got to ask her why she would do something like that to me."

"Well," Death said to me, "let's go back to that time in your life and check it out. Shall we?"

I was in the middle of telling him no, when we appeared inside the house that I despised with a passion.

"Why are we here?" I asked him in a rage. "I hated this place." Death didn't answer; he continued to float towards the living room. "I want to leave. I can't handle being in this place again."

"Just wait."

Sitting on the couch was my mother and her sister. My mother looked down at the floor while she sobbed silently. "I can't do this. She's my entire life, but I can't take care of her. My heart is breaking because now that I have my daughter, a dream I've had my whole life, I find out that I have this 'incurable disease'."

They were quiet for a moment before my aunt asked her "How long did they give you to live?"

"About a year, but I'm going to use my last year to work hard so that my daughter will have a better life than I did. Thank you Sister for offering to take care of her," the tears were sliding down her cheeks as she gave her a sad smile.

"Don't worry Sister. I'll take care of her as if she were my own. Just send me the money each month, and I will make sure she lacks for nothing."

I froze; I couldn't believe what I was hearing. My mother actually left me because she loved me. The realization hit me like a ton of bricks. She did love me. I felt as though a dark cloud that was suffocating me had lifted. I had this urge to hug my daughter and husband, to go back to where I was...but was that how this ended?

"So what now? Are you going to take me with you and my daughter has to go through losing her mother?"

"It really depends...Has this realization changed you, even in the slightest?"

I nodded, my eyes closing as I felt the tears start to build up. When I opened my eyes, I was leaning against the steering wheel, back in the driver's seat of my car. It took a while for me to understand that the car was on its side, and I was up against the wheel and the side window. In the distance, I could hear the sirens quickly approaching. Every day from now on, I will thank my lucky stars that I'm still here. I will see my life in this whole new perspective — thanks to this. I choked back a sob, hoping my mother knew how much I missed her and how much I wish she could see her grandchild. Maybe it was her that saved me this time...

Can't Think

A dark cloud above open skies

Shadows over the lives of many

Rain pours and ruins lives

Many fail to see the light

Laughter seeps out of their minds and only tears arise

Weak and disheartened, death is at their side

Feeling alone and departed

Society forgets they're alive

Some march on, some lose their minds

Depression strikes

Creating a maze for those whom it had in its grasp

Illusions rise

Paradise after life

Death being their only clasp

They let go and let depression be their demise

Multiple personality disorder is an illness where the person could have any number of different personalities that they might not even know about.

This story is of a letter describing the facts and events that change the character's life.

Story Three: My Final Letter

I wish I could say that I saw this coming. In fact, even today I cannot describe exactly what happened. It is hard to tell what is real and what is simply a dream.

I am writing this now as I sit in a cold, dark room — waiting for what will come. Even now, the messages will not stop. They continue to haunt me, and I have already begun to question my sanity. I have been caged in here for a week almost to the day; however, the hours have become cluttered and mixed together.

In order to make sense of this myself, I need to write out my story. I do not know how to start. One might say to start from the beginning, but the details are still fuzzy...I do remember, though, that it all started with a dream.

XxXxXxXxXxXxXxXxX

The dream was like a portal between my two worlds: a world that made no sense and a world where I was unable to control myself.

Every night I would fall asleep and wake up with little to no recollection of my evening. Things were not bad at first, losing just memory of my night; I only figured that it had to do with stress and absent mindedness.

I am getting ahead of myself, however. Let me go back and explain the "Official Day One". Maybe then I can put my dream into words.

XxXxXxXxXxXxXxXxX

"Day One" took place only a month ago. That was the day when I realized something was indeed wrong. It was the thirteenth of June, the last Friday before school was over. I had not been feeling well the week before, so I decided to start my summer vacation early. I figured my students could live without me for one day.

I woke up that morning as I would any other day. However, instead of rushing through my daily routine, I was able to ease through it.

Walking into my bathroom, I brightened up at the thought of a relaxing shower. That thought was banished from my mind when I finally looked up at the mirror. Instead of staring at my reflection, I was met with shards of glass and dark red pools of liquid surrounding the sink.

I stumbled out of the bathroom and into the den. Things were not better there. Pillows from the couch were thrown everywhere, ripped open. Books had been tossed from the bookshelf and sprawled haphazardly on the ground. The table had been flipped over, but all of these things seemed insignificant to what would be the oddest part. Carved into the entire eastern wall was a phrase that seemed so foreign to me.

"A clear and innocent conscience fears nothing."

It took up the entire wall with the way it was written. I remember the fear that nailed me to that spot. I was filled with a fright not knowing how this happened and if the person who carved it was still in my house. I immediately darted to my cell phone, intending on phoning the police.

The details after that are rather hazy now. The cops showed up thirty minutes later. Their office was swamped with an investigation into two missing professors at the local high school. This, of course, I knew. I had worked closely with the missing teachers.

The police surveyed the entire house. It seemed that they tore it apart even more than it was. Two detectives took pictures of the wall, ripped books, shredded pillows and every corner of the building. There were some investigators in the bathroom looking for fingerprints and collecting blood samples. Two officers, one male and one female, interrogated me about everything I knew, which was nothing.

Things went rather quickly after that. They took my prints to clear it from the set that they found. It took about three hours from the moment I woke up to when everyone finally left, and I was surprised at the speed it took them. Apparently they would call me if anything was found. It all left me confused; I figured that more would be done but that was it.

The rest of the day is unimportant to my tale. I was given the okay to clean everything up, so that is what I spent my day off doing. There was nothing I could do about the carving on the wall.

The following day was spent in fear that it might possibly happen again. I did not know that I was safe for the moment.

Two days later, I awoke from a dream, a strange one that has followed me to today. I was in a dark and cold place. At first, it seemed like I was searching for something or someone. Then, from behind me, stepped a figure.

His build seemed to make him masculine and he was nearly half a foot taller than me, which was not a great feat at my five foot seven inches. I did not notice the knife in his grasp until it was too late for me to do anything but wait.

"What do you want with me?" I asked. The voice I spoke with did not sound like my own.

He did not speak, he moved closer — slowly and quietly. I inched backwards and tried to put some distance between the two of us, but he shuffled forward faster.

He grabbed my arm and jerked me closer to him, slashing at my body with the weapon. I knew that I could not truly feel the pain, but my mind was able to fool my emotions and I screamed out.

The nightmare, for the most part, was reoccurring, haunting me every other night or so. Some nights, I saw farther into the dream, seeing up until the moment he killed me, with the memories plaguing my mind as I would wake.

The lingering thoughts of pain would follow after, making me feel like I was hurt. Was this lucid dreaming? I knew I was asleep, but there was nothing I could do to wake up or change the outcome.

The morning after I had the first dream, I was met with more writing and books sprawled everywhere. The phrase was written in a marker below the previous writing.

"Innocence is a kind of insanity"

This one made a tad more sense. It was a quote from a novel I had my students read during spring break. The books were scattered around the couch in some sort of fashion. I stared at the writing and then down at the books. There was something strange about the way they were placed. Then I understood.

All of the books were flipped upside down except one. It was the novel in which the quote was from. I gaped at the single object, afraid to go near it. It was obviously placed like that for a reason, and it was possible that I had fallen into a trap.

Sucking it up, I picked up the book. There had to be something about this particular book that made whoever did this leave it here. On the inside cover, "**DO NOT CALL THE POLICE.**" was written in all capitals. The writing continued on the following page, "**It is not safe. *YOU* are not safe.**"

The entire ordeal was beginning to frighten me. Whoever was doing this was able to enter my house without me waking and was now telling *me* to not call the police. I could heed the warning and keep this to myself, or I could ignore it totally and call the cops again.

But…what if what this person's saying is true? What if I am not safe?

It was too much for me to handle so early in the morning. I needed coffee.

XxXxXxXxXxXxXxXxX

An hour after I had woken up, I was sitting on the couch with a half drunk coffee cup in my hand. I had not moved anything other than the single book, leaving the mess still as it was.

Either decision that I ended up choosing could be dangerous. If I *do* call the police and I am truly not safe, any number of things could happen. Maybe the message was to warn me *of the police*.

However, if this whole thing was just a hoax, I could be in danger of whoever was doing this. It was clearly evident that the perpetrator was able to break into my home while I lay sleeping.

I ended up sitting in that same position for a couple hours, debating both sides. Finally I had chosen to listen to whatever this was. I would not call the cops. I needed to handle this on my own.

XxXxXxXxXxXxXxXxX

The days following my decision were different. Every message that popped up somewhere was another quote from a book or some warning. It was almost as if we were playing a game...a game in where I was risking my life.

I had begun keeping a journal of all the events that arose. Day after day something seemed to appear.

XxXxXxXxXxXxXxXxX

"Day Eighteen" was one of the scariest and strangest. Everything began the moment I woke up.

I had crawled out of bed at near noon to get ready for a day filled with nothing. We were still in the early stages of break, so I had nothing planned.

Walking into the bathroom, I finally noticed something. My hands and shirt were drenched in a red liquid, which I assumed was blood. I choked back a scream and searched for some wound on my body. Finding none, I dashed back to my bed. Lying by my pillow was a single severed hand, sliced off at the wrist.

Coming to my senses, I backed away as quickly as possible and went towards the phone. I needed to ignore the voice in my head reminding me of the warning to *not* call the police and dialed '9-1-1'.

XxXxXxXxXxXxXxXxX

The police arrived ten minutes after the call. It was the same team from last time I called, maybe a coincidence.

I showed them to the room and gestured towards the amputated limb. The same two detectives sat me down to recall my story. I listened to the voice now, telling them only of what happened today. When they asked if any more messages where found, I immediately shook my head. They glanced at each other then went back to writing every detail down.

As they walked away, I was able to overhear their conversation.

"We cannot make an arrest at this point. Even though something like this was found, we have no evidence who placed it there. The defense would argue that that this could be a set-up. The fact that we were already here for another possible break-in raises the chances in that."

"Then we keep searching. We will have someone keep an eye on this house."

They ended up not taking me in for more questioning, but I figured that this was not over. They bagged the hand in hopes of fingerprinting who it belonged to. The bed sheets were also taken as well as the t-shirt I had been wearing.

Listening in on the conversation I knew that this would not be the last time they would be here.

XxXxXxXxXxXxXxXxX

"Day Twenty-three" was the end of it all. I had not received any more 'messages' since the day before the hand showed up in my bed. I figured that maybe it was all over.

It is never that easy.

I was unable to wake up peacefully. There was a terrible pounding at the door, rousing me from sleep. Just as I was climbing out of bed, the door was kicked in and five officers wielding weapons rushed forward.

"We have...warrant...your arrest."

I blinked and stared up at the man charging towards me. His words seemed jumbled in my head.

"You have the...be silent...say can and will...you have the right...one will be appointed..."

I tried to blink again but my eyelids were too heavy. Just as they cuffed my hands, I blacked out.

XxXxXxXxXxXxXxXxX

That was how I ended up here in this jail cell. Most of the facts still do not match up.

It was not until several days after my arrival here that I pieced together the details. I was brought to a therapist where I was diagnosed with Multiple Personality Disorder, or Dissociative Identity Disorder. There seemed to be another 'me' inside of my body.

There was no break-in. No particular person was or is after me, that much I am sure. It was only another side of me that was trying to warn the leading 'me' of danger that was coming towards me...or us.

The reason for my arrest was later explained to me. The police located the body that the severed hand belonged to. The only prints near the scene belonged to me. The body that was found was the teacher that had gone missing over a month earlier.

Did I kill her? I truly do not know. I do not believe so; otherwise I would not have tried so hard to warn my other self.

It makes sense now, thinking that someone was after me. Except it was more than only one. Do I know why? No. Fighting against the police is hopeless and futile.

I only wish to know why it happened, to me of all people. I am a normal person, trying to live a normal life.

Well, it is time for me to leave. The warden was kind enough to slip me a pen and paper to set my story straight. I do not know what will come of me now, but I am sure that it will not be good.

Goodbye,

– Jaden Johnson

Is This Me?

Sometimes I wonder why I am like this

Born into this body with others living in it

All I can do is sit back and watch the world go by

For I don't know which things are an illusion

And which are reality

These other versions of me

How many are there exactly

It's a constant fight sometimes

A battle for dominance

Some people like to say they know how it feels to fight yourself

But compare that to my situation and you can tell

Tell the difference of what my world is like

To how you see me through your eyes

Is nothing compared to mine

I look at myself all the time

Judging and questioning if I'll be fine

www.ingramcontent.com/pod-product-compliance
Ingram Content Group UK Ltd.
Pitfield, Milton Keynes, MK11 3LW, UK
UKHW041903190726
13854UKWH00003B/1053

9 781304 299512